This book belongs to

DA Niella
Cohen

Happiness

Wisdom

Cocoa

Beauty Sleep

This is the story of Crystal Clean,

the sleeping daughter of a king and queen.

On every page, can you guess what?

There's a feather duster for you to spot.

Sleeping Beauty

Nick and Claire Page

Illustrations by Sara Baker

make
believe
ideas

Once a king and queen
held a party on the green,
to celebrate their baby.
They called her Crystal Clean.

They were thrilled to bits!
The king did the splits.
The queen served lots of crackers
with lots of cheesy bits.

Among the many guests
to welcome the princess
were seven kindly fairies,
who came to bless.

Mary Beth

Good Dental Care

Mary Jo

Mary

Beauty

Wisdom

Goodness

A scary fairy came.
Griselda was her name.
She hadn't been invited
but walked in all the same.

"A curse!" Griselda said.
"A curse upon her head!
She'll be stabbed by a spindle.
Your baby will be dead!"

"No need for any fears,"
the youngest fairy cheers.
"I'll change this curse, instead
she will sleep for a hundred years."

The queen warns Crystal Clean,
each year till she's sixteen,
"Don't ever touch a spindle.
You don't know where it's been."

But then one night,
much to her delight,
the princess found a secret tower,
and there, shining bright . . .

15

a spinning wheel she found,
spinning round and round.
She pricked her little finger
and fell to the ground.

DO NOT TOUCH

17

You couldn't hear a peep.
Everybody fell asleep.
The place was filled with snoring
and dreaming deep.

A hundred years went by.
The ivy climbed so high,
you'd never know the castle
stood nearby.

Then along the forest floor,
comes a prince, who finds the door.
He cuts through thorns and roses
and thinks he hears a snore.

WEED
BE GONE

The castle's in a mess.
The prince finds the princess.
He falls in love, he kisses her,
and she wakes up! Success!

DO NOT
TOUCH

23

He marries Crystal Clean,
and on the village green
they hold the biggest party
that you have ever seen!

Ready to tell

Oh no! Some of the pictures from this story have been mixed up! Can you retell the story and point to each picture in the correct order?

26

27

Picture dictionary

Encourage your child to read these words from the story and gradually develop his or her basic vocabulary.

castle

fairy

needle

party

presents

pricks

prince

princess

spinning wheel

Key words

Here are some key words used in context. Help your child to use other words from the border in simple sentences.

The king **and** queen have a baby girl.

She will prick her finger.

A prince finds the castle.

He kisses **the** princess.

They hold a big party.

Make a spinning star

You might not have a spinning wheel at home, but you can still weave a colourful woollen star. It's so simple!

You will need

2 sticks of equal length, such as chopsticks or cocktail sticks • lengths of wool in different colours

What to do

1 Form a cross with the sticks, then use the wool to tie them together, finishing with a knot. Do not cut the wool.
2 Keeping the wool taut, weave it under and around each stick in turn. The circle will gradually get bigger as you work towards the end of the sticks.
3 Change colours every so often by tying in a new strand of wool whenever you feel like it.
4 Experiment with weaving the wool in and out in different ways.
5 If, when you have finished, you have any gaps, try weaving in lengths of ribbon. You can also try making little shapes out of card or wood and glueing them onto your woollen star.
6 To hang up your star, tie a length of wool through the woven wool at the top of one stick, make a loop, and knot it. Pin up your star and let it spin!

This igloo book belongs to:

....

igloobooks

Written by Joff Brown
Illustrated by Gareth Conway

Copyright © 2017 Igloo Books Ltd

An imprint of Bonnier Publishing USA
251 Park Avenue South, New York, New York 10010
Manufactured in China. HUN001 1117
10 9 8 7 6 5 4 3 2 1

Library of Congress Cataloging-in-Publication
Data is available upon request.

ISBN 978-1-4998-8039-7
IglooBooks.com
bonnierpublishingusa.com

My First Treasury of
DINOSAUR
Tales

igloobooks

CONTENTS

The Big Day Out

Gordon the Brachiosaurus was the biggest, nicest dinosaur in town. He would do anything for his friends. One day, Gordon and his buddies were getting ready to visit Prehistoric Park, the most exciting theme park ever.

"I've hurt my foot," said Gordon's friend, Summer.
"I'll never make it to the bus for Prehistoric Park."
"Get on my back," said Gordon. "I'll carry you there."
Summer hopped on and soon they were there.

7

"Hey, Gordon," said the bus driver. "A wheel on the bus is broken. We'll never get to Prehistoric Park unless we change it. Can you help?" Gordon summoned all his strength and lifted the bus while the driver changed the wheel.

Gordon was about to get on the bus when he saw his
friend Becky crying. "My ball is stuck up a tree," she said.
Gordon reached up with his long neck and grabbed the ball for Becky.
"Come on, Gordon!" called his friends. "We're leaving for Prehistoric Park!"

Gordon ran to the bus. He pushed and squeezed and tried to get in, but the door was too small. Gordon couldn't fit.

"Goodbye," he said, walking off sadly. "Have fun without me."

Later, Gordon was sitting miserably at home
when he heard a BEEP-BEEP coming from outside.
It was the bus with an enormous chair tied to the back of it.
"We made this for you," Gordon's friends said. "Hop aboard!"

Gordon jumped on and the bus sped to Prehistoric Park. When they got there, Gordon squeezed on to the roller coaster, taking up a whole carriage. "Whoo!" he cried as the roller coaster zoomed around the track.

Gordon and his friends had an amazing day at Prehistoric Park.
"The rides were great, but the best one of all was the ride here
on the bus," said Gordon, "thanks to my brilliant friends."

13

My mom's the best, she beats the rest.
She'll always be my buddy.
We play outdoors and she doesn't mind,
When I get really muddy.

The cakes she bakes all taste so good,
They make my tummy rumble.
Her cupcakes rule, but best of all,
Is her awesome apple crumble.

15

When rain and lightning fill the sky,
And the thunder starts to crash,
We find a puddle and jump right in,
To make a great big splash.

We run back home for cookies,
And hot milk to keep us warm,
Then, at bedtime, I get tucked in,
By the world's most magic mom!

Trey's Tremendous Tail

Trey the Diplodocus had the biggest tail in town. Everywhere that Trey went, his tail went, too. It stuck out behind him and was always causing lots of trouble, especially for his friends.

One day, at the playground, Trey spun around on the merry-go-round and fell off. His enormous tail knocked his friends flying. "Ouch!" they cried. "Be careful next time, Trey."

19

Trey went to play at the water hole with his friend Lucy. He bent down to drink some cool water and his tail shot in the air. "ARGH!" cried Lucy as she was scooped up by his tail. "Put me down, Trey, I'm scared."

Trey saw his friends playing basketball at the park. "Can I play?" asked Trey.
"No way. Your tail is too much trouble," his friends said.
"I can't help that my tail is so big," said Trey sadly. "I was born like this."

At school the next day, it started to snow. The snow got really deep. "Oh, no. We can't get home now," said Trey's friends. Suddenly, Trey had an idea. He went outside and swished his tail from side to side.

Swish, swoosh went the snow. "Look!" cried Lucy.
"Trey has cleared a path for us. We can go home."
Everyone cheered. "You're our hero, Trey!"
they cried. At last, Trey's tail was out of trouble.

I Can Do It, Dad!

I always like to help my dad,
He loves it when I join in.
Wherever we go, he makes funny faces,
And I just can't help but grin.

When Dad competes at basketball,
I always stand and cheer.
I yell, "Go, Dad, you're number one!"
For all the crowd to hear.

25

When Dad does his handiwork,
I'll be there in a rush.
I splash the paint on everywhere,
Except for on the brush.

I wrote a story just for Dad,
And he's the hero, too.
He saves the world from aliens,
There's nothing Dad can't do!

27

Sean the Show-off

Sean the Spinosaurus was the biggest show-off in school.
"I'm the best at everything," Sean would say to his friends.
"Stop bragging all the time," his friends would reply.

One day, in gym class, the dinosaurs were jumping on a trampoline. "I'm the best at trampolining," said Sean. He bounced up really high on the trampoline. *Boing, boing, boing!* All his friends went flying off.

After, it was time for music class. "I'm the best at music," said Sean. When he blew into his trumpet, it was so loud, everybody dropped their instruments in surprise. "Stop being a show-off," his friends said.

On the basketball court, Sean grabbed the basketball every time.
"Pass it to us!" yelled his friends. Instead, Sean barged past everyone
and dunked the ball into the basket to score.

The next day, the teacher announced a special treat for the class.
"It's time for a swimming lesson," he said. Everyone clapped and cheered,
but Sean went very quiet. He didn't know how to swim.

Everyone jumped in the pool, while Sean stood on the side, shivering.
"I don't like it. I want to go home!" he cried. Sean's friends were amazed.
"We thought you were the best at everything," they said.

"If I'm not the best, then nobody will like me!" Sean wailed.
"Don't be silly," his friends said. "We like you because of YOU,
even though you're a show-off. We'll help you to learn to swim."

34

At the next lesson, Sean's friends gave him a pair of swim wings and goggles. Soon, Sean was splishing and splashing around. "I may not be the best at everything," he said. "But I definitely do have the best friends ever!"

Dino Dance-o

Dennis loved to dance. He danced at home. He danced in school.
He even danced at the park. "Go away, Dennis," said his friends.
"You're making us look silly."

"I'm practicing for a big dance competition," said Dennis, suddenly feeling shy. Dennis's friends liked playing soccer and skating. "Dancing is for girls," they said. Dennis felt very upset.

On his way home, Dennis looked at the poster for the dance competition. "My friends might think I'm silly," he thought. "But I'll practice and practice and I'll win that competition."

It was the day of the competition. Dennis stepped on to the stage. Suddenly, he felt very nervous. He couldn't move. The audience fell silent. "I can't do it," thought Dennis. Then, he heard familiar voices. . . .

"You can do it, Dennis!" cried his friends. Suddenly, Dennis began to move. He tapped and swayed. He shuffled and shimmied. Dennis even stood on his head. "Hooray!" cheered the audience.

Dennis was so good that he won first prize. "Well done, Dennis," said his friends. "Sorry we were mean to you. Now we think dancing is cool." Dennis had never been happier.

You and Me

When we moved houses, the streets were so strange.
I left all my friends when we made our big change.
"You'll make new friends," said Mom, but I didn't feel good.
I was all on my own in a new neighborhood.

42

Then I peeked over the fence and I saw you playing.
"Hey, buddy, come over," I heard your little voice saying.
I pushed you on the swing and you went up really high.
You told me I'm super fun and a pretty cool guy.

"Let's play pretend," you said, without any fuss.
"We'll make a special den just for the two of us.
We'll be fierce pirates in a fortress today.
We'll dig up buried treasure and hide it away."

After that, every day, we both played together.
We always went outside, whatever the weather.
As long as I'm with you, the fun will never end,
Because you're fantastic and my very best friend.

Sing-a-saurus

Colin loved to sing. The problem was, he couldn't sing very well.
One morning, he woke up early. "This is the perfect day for a song,"
he said. So he sang at the top of his voice. "LA-LA-LA-LAAAA!"
"Shhh," said his little brother, Charlie. "What a racket."

When Colin went shopping with his mommy, he burst into song again. "LA-LA-LA-LAAAA!" he sang. All the other shoppers dropped their groceries in surprise. "Go away, Colin!" they cried, putting their fingers in their ears. "You can't sing."

Colin was fed up. He wished everyone would like his singing.
He ran to the library to look for a special book on how to sing. When he
arrived, the library was very quiet. Colin couldn't help it, he just HAD to sing.
"LA-LA-LA-LA-LA-LA-LAAA!" he wailed, annoying the other dinosaurs.

Colin couldn't seem to impress anyone. He sat outside, feeling glum.
"No one likes me," he said sadly. "Everyone hates my singing."
"Not everyone," said Farmer Fred as he walked past the library.
"I've got the perfect job for you, Colin."

49

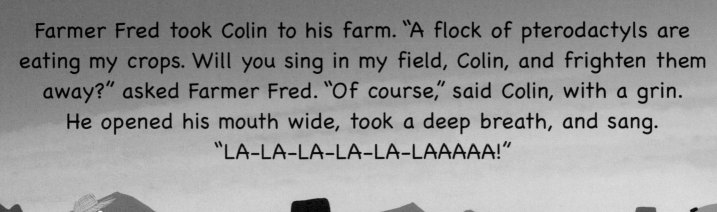

Farmer Fred took Colin to his farm. "A flock of pterodactyls are eating my crops. Will you sing in my field, Colin, and frighten them away?" asked Farmer Fred. "Of course," said Colin, with a grin. He opened his mouth wide, took a deep breath, and sang. "LA-LA-LA-LA-LA-LAAAAA!"

When the pterodactyls heard Colin, they shrieked and flew away. "Perfect!" cried Farmer Fred. "Sing as much as you like. That will keep the pests away." So Colin spent all day singing to his heart's content. Everyone was happy, except for the pterodactyls!

51

Hungry Herbie

Jason's cousin, Herbie, was coming to visit today. Herbie liked to eat anything and everything! "Don't let him eat my special cupcakes," Mom warned Jason as Herbie raced into the kitchen.

Jason suddenly had a bright idea. He grabbed a plate of yummy cookies to distract Herbie from the cupcakes. "Mmmm, cookies!" cried Herbie, following Jason as he ran upstairs.

"Those cookies should keep him busy," said Jason, but when he turned around, the plate was already empty. Herbie had disappeared. Jason followed the trail of cookie crumbs back downstairs.

Herbie was in the kitchen. "Oh, no! You've eaten my mom's cupcakes," cried Jason as Herbie grabbed more food from the fridge. "Come on. Let's go outside and play so you don't eat anything else."

Jason led Herbie into the garden and they played hide-and-seek. Herbie scampered off while Jason counted to ten. When Jason opened his eyes again, he couldn't find his little cousin anywhere.

56

Just then, there was a CRUNCH-CRUNCH-CRUNCH! Jason followed the noise to Dad's vegetable patch and found Herbie feasting on lettuce and carrots. "Stop it! They're Dad's prized vegetables," cried Jason.

Jason's mom appeared at the back door. "I've made more cupcakes," she called. "Mmmm, cupcakes!" cried Herbie, dropping the vegetables and running inside. "Wait for me," said Jason.

They sat down to eat. "Would you like a cupcake, Herbie?" asked Jason, but Herbie snored. "He's gone to sleep," said Mom. Jason giggled. "Herbie's not hungry anymore," he said, taking a bite of a delicious cupcake. "But I am!"

Better Together

When I'm playing alone, I get lonely,
So I run to my sister and say,
"Come on, Sis, let's be ninjas or pirates.
It's a better-with-two kind of day!"

60

In the park, we see who can swing higher.
Then we race to the slide at a run.

We bounce on each end of the seesaw.
Playing together is so much fun.

We both like singing and dancing.
Sometimes we put on a play.
If you do it alone, then it's scary,
But with two, all my fears go away.

We play inside and outside.
We play whatever the weather.
Mom says we are double the trouble,
When we are playing together.

My Dad's Dynamite

I really love my dad because,
He's always there by my side.
At the park, he helps me,
On to the monkey bars and slide.

When we go out bowling,
Dad helps me with the ball.
I knock down one or two pins,
But Dad always hits them all.

When it's warm and sunny,
Dad's the barbecuing king.
From ribs and chops to sausages,
He flame-grills anything.

66

There's nothing broken that Dad can't fix.
He's always DIY-ing.
His shelves and chairs are very wonky,
But it doesn't stop him trying.

Sometimes when I've been good at school,
Dad lets me stay up late.
Mom says I should be fast asleep,
But me, I think it's great!

He reads me all the books I love,
When I'm tucked in at night.
That's why Dad is number one.
He really is dynamite!

I Can Help, Mom!

My mom and I love riding bikes,
And playing on the swing.
I water all the flowers she plants,
And help with everything.

Today, it's my mom's birthday,
We're making a yummy cake.
The flour and cream go everywhere,
We really love to bake.

We go on great adventures,
Rock climbing is so much fun.
I help my mom climb really high,
And show her how it's done.

When Mom's tired and needs a rest,
She sinks into her comfy chair.
I sit on her lap and hug her tight,
To show how much I care.

73

The Cretaceous Cup

It was the grand final of the Cretaceous Cup. The Dinky Dinos were super excited to have made it so far. Dan, Dexter, Daisy, Debbie, Dennis, and Dean ran on to the pitch. Their opponents were the Jurassic Giants.

The Giants thundered towards the Dinos. The ground shook. "They'll squash us!" cried Dennis, hiding behind Dan. The whistle blew and the crowd cheered. The match had begun.

Dennis made a dash for the ball. He dribbled it and passed the ball to Dexter. Just then, Greg, one of the Giants's strikers, sprinted toward Dexter. He flattened him with a tackle.

Greg ran all the way up the pitch, knocking the Dinos flying.
He slammed the ball into the net. The Giants were just too big to stop.
They were already winning and by halftime, the score was 3–0.

"We don't stand a chance. We're just too dinky," said Dexter in the locker room. "No, we're not," said Dennis. "We might be little, but we're very fast. We need to speed up. Let's go!"

The second-half whistle blew. Dennis passed the ball to Dan, who quickly dodged a tackle. The Dinos nipped in and out. They zipped this way and that. The Giants just couldn't keep up.

Dennis twisted and turned, right under the Giants's feet. He passed
the ball to Dexter, who dribbled the ball to the other end of the pitch.
He kicked . . . and scored! The Dinos' supporters roared with glee.

The final whistle blew. The Dinky Dinos had won 5–3. They all cheered and hoisted the Cretaceous Cup into the air. "We might be little," said Dan with a laugh, "but that sure helped us in the end!"

Groovy Grandparents

It was the school holidays and Jake was going to stay with his grandparents. "It's going to be soooooooooooo boring," moaned Jake. "All they'll do is sleep in front of the TV and make me eat boring food."

When Jake arrived at Granny and Grandpa's house, there was loud music coming from the living room. "They're playing my favorite band!" cried Jake. "They're my favorite band, too," said Granny, doing a funny dance. "Wow," gasped Jake. "That's amazing!"

Afterward, Grandpa brought out a cool, stripy skateboard. "Let's go to the skate park," he said. "You can't skate, Grandpa," said Jake, confused. "Yes, I can," laughed Grandpa. "I'm a super skating champion."

Sure enough, Grandpa whizzed through the skate park, whooshing up all the ramps. Everyone watched in amazement as Grandpa pulled off trick after trick. "Wow!" cried Jake. "You're the best grandpa ever."

When Jake was worn out, they went home. "Granny has a surprise dinner waiting," said Grandpa. "I bet it's boring beans on toast," replied Jake.

The surprise dinner was a huge box of yummy pizza. "Mmm," said Jake, with his mouth full. "Thank you. You're the best granny ever."

When Dad came to pick Jake up the next day, Jake didn't want to leave.
"Come back with me," he said jokingly to Granny and Grandpa.
"You could teach Mom and Dad a thing or two."

My Funny Family

My family's the greatest, it's full of funny folk.
My dad's a cheeky prankster who loves a silly joke.
My mom's so sweet and quiet, until we make a noise,
Then she yells above the din, "QUIET, GIRLS AND BOYS!"

My uncle Jim's a racer and his car is super speedy.
My auntie Jenny loves to bake, it's why we're all so greedy!
My grandpa's an astronomer, he charts the Milky Way.
My granny knits, at megaspeed, a sweater every day.

My sister's neat and tidy. She likes to keep things clean.
My brother always makes a mess, the worst you've ever seen.
He loves to get her muddy by splashing into puddles,
But they both love the baby, who likes their great big cuddles.

We're all so very different, I'm sure that's plain to see,
But we all love a party with the whole big family.
We may seem pretty funny, but there's one thing we all claim,
A family would be very boring if everyone was the same!

Donnie Hates the Dark

Donnie HATED the dark. One night, he was camping outside with his friend Amy, but only because she had insisted. "What a lovely night," she said, sitting on the grass. "I'm not coming out of the tent," said Donnie anxiously. "There might be monsters in the dark."

Donnie noticed something shining in the night sky. "What's that? Is it an alien spaceship?" he whispered, terrified. "Of course not. It's just the moon," said Amy, smiling. Donnie peeked out of the tent. "I suppose it's a very nice moon," he said. "But I'm still staying inside, where it's safe."

Then Donnie spotted some little lights in the sky. "What are those? Are they the eyes of monsters?" he asked nervously. "Don't be silly," said Amy. "They're just the twinkly stars." Donnie poked his whole head out of the tent. "Wow!" he cried. "Look at how bright they are."

Donnie saw some tiny creatures glowing by a bush. "ARGH! What are those little mutants?" he cried. "They're not mutants, they're just fireflies," laughed Amy. Donnie slowly stepped out of the tent. "Amazing," he said. "Hmmm, maybe there aren't any monsters in the dark, after all."

"Now that you're outside let's have a midnight feast,"
said Amy, toasting a marshmallow. "Unless you're still scared?"
"Nope," said Donnie. "With the moon, stars, and fireflies, the dark
is nothing to be afraid of. In fact, I think it's really cool."